STEWART'S TREE

A Book for Brothers and Sisters
When a Baby Dies Shortly after Birth

WRITTEN AND ILLUSTRATED BY

Cathy Campbell

Jessica Kingsley Publishers
London and Philadelphia

First published in 2018
by Jessica Kingsley Publishers
73 Collier Street
London N1 9BE, UK
and
400 Market Street, Suite 400
Philadelphia, PA 19106, USA

www.jkp.com

Library of Congress Cataloging in Publication Data
A CIP catalog record for this book is available from the Library of Congress

British Library Cataloguing in Publication Data
A CIP catalogue record for this book is available from the British Library

ISBN 978 1 78592 399 9
eISBN 978 1 78450 762 6

Printed and bound in China

Ellen was waiting for something special.

She wasn't going to her favourite place,

...or to the park.

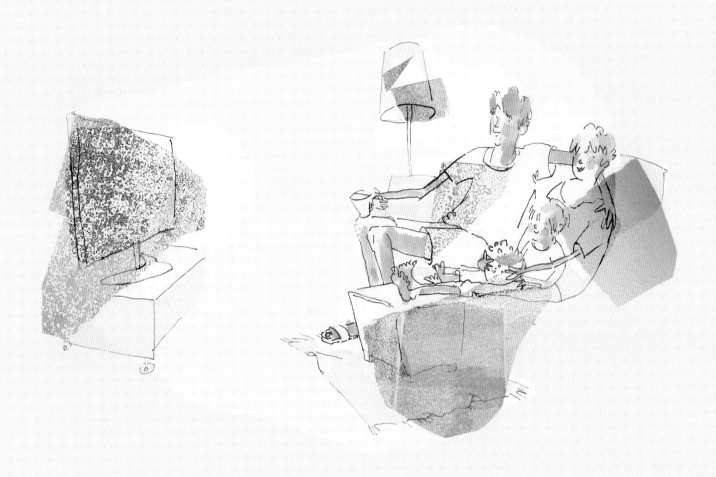

And it wasn't movie night either!

Granny and Papa were coming to stay,

and they had brought a special gift, because…

…Ellen had a new baby brother called Stewart.

She couldn't wait for him to come home!

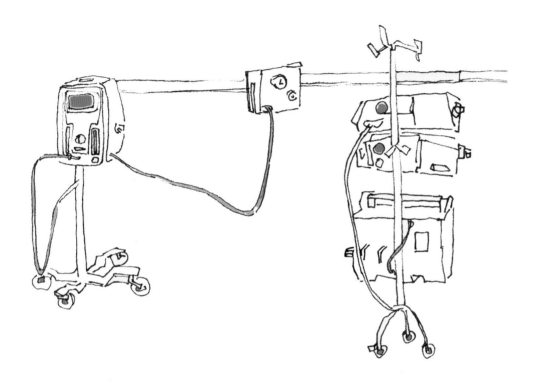

But something was wrong with Stewart.
Ellen thought his cot looked like a spaceship.

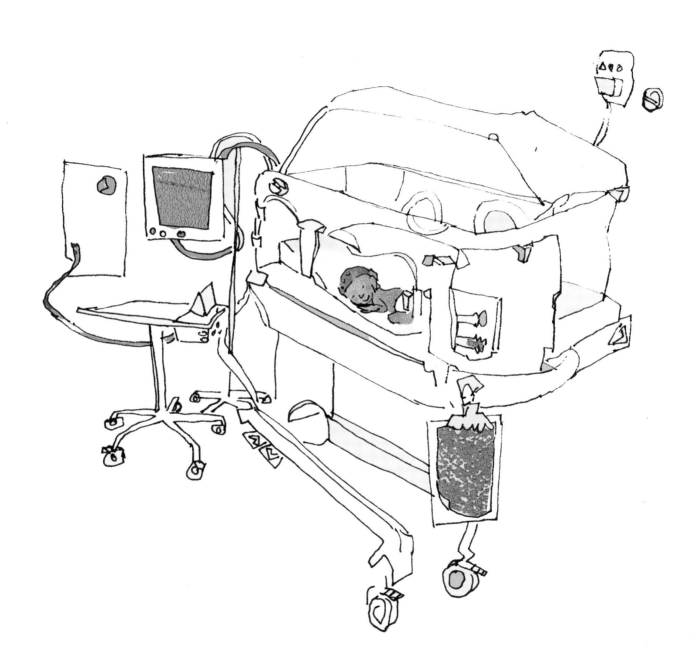

The doctor said it was alright for them to take Stewart outside for a walk.
It was raining and a little bit sunny too.

Dad said Stewart could feel the wind.

Mum said he could smell the rain. Ellen thought he could
feel the warmth of the autumn sunshine.

At home the phone rang AGAIN!
"They've lost the baby," Granny said.

Ellen thought, "I'll look for him."

But she couldn't find him anywhere.

She wondered if he'd gone to the moon in his spaceship.

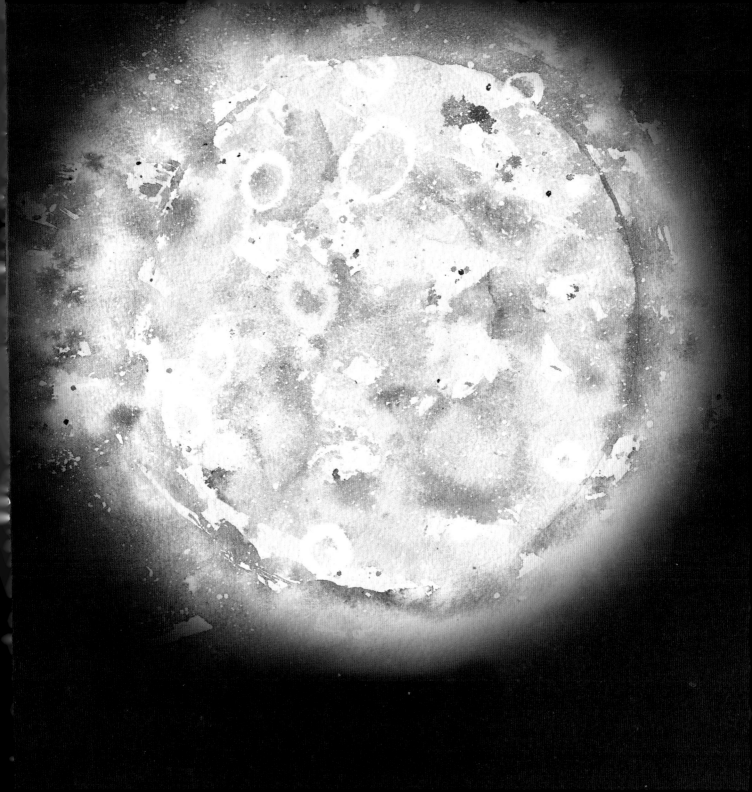

People came with vegetable soup,

but Ellen didn't like vegetables!

Lots of cards arrived, but it wasn't Ellen's birthday.
Maybe they were for Stewart…

But Ellen didn't know where he was.

Dad said that Stewart wasn't lost. He said that he was dead, which meant he wasn't alive any more. He couldn't feel the wind, or smell the rain, and he couldn't feel the warmth of the autumn sunshine. Mum said it was because he wasn't strong enough to live outside her tummy. She said he would never be forgotten because he is our family.

Ellen helped Dad to plant a little tree.

Mum said the birds would love to eat the juicy red cherries.

Ellen knew it would always be her favourite tree and it would help her to remember Stewart.

I wrote *Stewart's Tree* primarily for Ellen Mackay, whose little brother Stewart died of a condition called hypoplastic left heart syndrome. As the project developed it became clear that this book could help other families, too.

With special thanks to Vivienne and David Mackay and family.

This book is dedicated to

Douglas Stewart Mackay

25.09.2000 – 7.10.2000

and

Caitlin Murray

16.04.1999 – 24.04.1999

GUIDE FOR ADULTS

Telling anyone that a baby has died or is unlikely to live is always hard. Telling children is especially difficult. Each family and each child are different. There is no one right way to talk to a child. What you say will depend on the child's age, their ability to understand, and the questions they ask.

WHAT TO SAY

Young children do not usually need complicated or deep explanations. A simple and honest explanation is often enough. It's probably best to start by saying that the baby has died, even if the child is too young to fully understand what that means. You could also tell the child the baby's sex and name if you have chosen one.

You could suggest they draw or paint a picture to say goodbye to the baby. If you want to involve them further, you could ask if they would like to come to the hospital to see the baby and to say goodbye. If you will be bringing the baby home, you could explain that this is so that the whole family can say goodbye together. It's generally a good idea to explain that you are very sad because the baby has died and that it's OK to feel unhappy and to cry when sad things happen. It's also important to explain to younger children that you are not upset because of something they have done, and that it's not their fault.

It's important to choose carefully the words you use to explain that the baby has died. Children tend to take things very literally. Some words and phrases may confuse younger children. Saying that the baby is "asleep" or "sleeping" may make a child afraid of going to sleep. Using the words "lost" or "gone" instead of "died" may make a child frightened of getting lost themselves. Some children may think that if the baby is lost or gone, he or she could be found again or come back.

Saying "the baby wasn't well" may worry a child later when he or she is ill. Instead you might say, "The baby wasn't strong enough or big enough to live outside Mummy's tummy."

You may also want to think about the way a young child might react to phrases such as "the baby is an angel," or "the baby is with the angels." This could cause problems if, later, someone says to the child "you are an angel…" or "be an angel…" An explanation such as "God wanted the baby to be with Him" might frighten a child who thinks that God might want him or her as well.

It's usually better to keep things short and clear and not try to say too much at any one time. If a child wants to know more they will probably ask questions, as long as they feel it is alright to ask.

PRE-SCHOOL CHILDREN

Very young children are unlikely to understand completely what has happened but will react to the changes in the atmosphere around them. They are especially sensitive to changes in the people they depend on and are closest to. Even if they know words such as dead or die, most children under the age of five or six find it hard to understand that death is permanent. Some may not react to what you tell them straight away. You may need to explain more than once.

Younger children, especially, will usually focus on how the death affects them, rather than how it's affecting you. Younger children are also likely to find it hard to put their feelings into words. They may express their distress through changes in their behaviour.

MEMENTOES AND MEMORY BOXES

Many parents collect mementoes such as photos, hand and foot prints, copies of scans, a lock of hair, cot tags and name bracelets. These can be stored in a memory box or book. Brothers and sisters might want to add something of their own to the box or book. Depending on their age, they could do a drawing or painting, or write a poem or a letter. Some children might want to give the baby a cuddly toy which could be placed in the coffin or kept in the memory box. An older child might want to help make a memory box for the family or to make one themselves.

This is a short edited extract from **Supporting children when a baby has died**, *published by SANDS Stillbirth and Neonatal Death Charity. The full booklet is available on the SANDS website at https://www.uk-sands.org/support/bereavement-support/supporting-children-when-baby-has-died and contains further information on supporting children and family life after the death of a baby at or shortly after birth, including advice on the longer term. The information has been reproduced here by kind permission of the charity.*

Sands
Stillbirth & neonatal death charity